The Taste Bud PLEDGE

I promise to keep my mind open and my fork ready, to try each new food at least two times and share what's on my plate when someone doesn't have enough.

....

Official Taste Bud

Kalamata's
KITCHEN
À la Kalamata

For my mother, who taught me about home, and Sandra,
who helped me build one of my own.

—Eric Ripert

We would like to thank our Le Bernardin family for their encouragement,
support, and flexibility in growing our business, and all of our
professional Taste Buds for continuing to inspire us with their stories.

—The Kalamata's Kitchen team

Published by Kalamata's Kitchen
kalamataskitchen.com

Edited and designed by Girl Friday Productions
girlfridayproductions.com

Text: Sarah Thomas
Illustration: Jo Edwards
Interior & cover design: Pulp + Wire and Paul Barrett

Hardcover ISBN: 9781732212626

First Edition

Printed in the United States of America

Featuring Her Taste Buds

Al Dente and Chef Eric Ripert

Deliciously written by Sarah Thomas & Illustrated by Jo Edwards

SOMETHING DELICIOUS

was happening in Kalamata's kitchen.

Earlier that day, Kalamata's mama had chop-chop-chopped lots of fresh veggies for **pistou soup** while Kalamata happily removed bright-green basil leaves from their stems.

The smell was so fresh, so full, so **everywhere** in the kitchen. Mama's chopped veggies and lots of other good-smelling herbs were simmering away in a pot.

Kalamata couldn't help but daydream about her bright, beautiful basil. "Is this what the color GREEN smells like?" she wondered.

Kalamata was just about to write a poem about it, when the doorbell rang.

Chef Eric was here to visit! And what a treat—he brought his son Adrien with him.

"*Bonjour, Kalamata!*
I can see and smell that you're very busy in here!"

"Yes, Chef, we are. But you've come a little too early to hear my poem about *green*—it's about basil, but also about Al Dente."

"I can't wait to hear that, Kalamata! This **beautiful green smell** is one of my favorites. It reminds me of when I was a little boy in Provence, in France, and if I close my eyes, I can almost imagine that I'm there."

"I wish we could go there too," said Adrien.

"Me too!" said Kalamata wistfully.

"You know, Adrien and I like to travel to different countries every weekend by creating our own restaurant at home and learning about food that people eat all over the world. You don't always have to leave your kitchen to travel to places far away . . ." Chef Eric said, winking at Kalamata.

Kalamata knew this very well.

Most grown-ups didn't know, but Kalamata's kitchen was magical. Under her table, Kalamata and Al Dente had gone on many adventures to fantastical faraway places, and now, Chef Eric and Adrien were going to join them too.

"Tonight, Kalamata's kitchen will be a new French restaurant!" announced Adrien proudly. *"Fantastique!"* exclaimed Chef Eric. "I'll be the chef. And, Kalamata, you'll be my sous-chef and help me prepare our meal. Adrien, you will be in charge of the dining room."

"And Al Dente can do the dishes!" said Kalamata, giggling.

The Taste Buds got to work right away. While Chef Eric and Kalamata washed the rosy-red tomatoes, Adrien designed their menus.

"What should we call our restaurant?" asked Adrien.

"Maison de la Dente? Or Chez Taste Bud?" suggested Kalamata.

How about **"À la Kalamata?"** Adrien offered. The whole team agreed that it was perfect—*parfait!* But not that kind of parfait, Al!

As they decorated the menus, the sounds of Chef Eric chopping and whisking, and the soft simmering of the soup pot filled the room like music.

"Kalamata, help me tear up these herbs. My grandmother had a beautiful garden in Provence. It was full of **rosemary** and **thyme** and **lavender**, and whenever I smell these crushed herbs, I remember their fragrance surrounding me as I ran through her garden."

Kalamata breathed in the earthy, herby smells and flew through Grandma's **gorgeous green garden.**

Sous-chef Kalamata and Chef Eric scooped the juicy middles out of the tomatoes, then filled them with chopped garlic, basil, and the savory good-smelling herbs. They covered the stuffed tomatoes with bread crumbs, and then slid their **tomates farcies** into the oven.

Together, Kalamata and Adrien set out the plates, with the fork to the left of the plate, and the knife and spoon to the right. They placed water glasses near each knife for Adrien and Kalamata and an extra-fancy glass for the grown-ups. They neatly set a napkin on each plate, and finally, their wonderfully drawn menus on top. Chef Eric lit a candle, and the team stood back to admire their work.

À la Kalamata was beautiful. The table had rarely looked prettier, or more inviting.

The smell of the toasty tomatoes under their bread crumb blankets enveloped them all.

"Kalamata, Adrien, thank you for creating this perfect Provençal restaurant with me," said Chef Eric happily. "I feel like a little boy again!"

"Thank you for taking us with you, Chef," said Kalamata gratefully. "I can't wait to tell Mama about our tasty trip to France!"

The team made all the last-minute checks and decided that every detail was perfect.

À la Kalamata was open for business!

Just then, Mama came back into the kitchen. She gasped with delight at the sight of the pretty table, all set up for dinner. "Kalamata! Adrien! How lovely this looks! Where did you all go today?"

Chef Eric smiled at Kalamata and started serving up their delicious meal. Kalamata opened her arms wide.

"Welcome to Provence, Mama—and *bienvenue* to À la Kalamata!"

RECIPE

Get going with a grown-up! You can make Chef Eric's *tomates farcies* at home too. Share a picture of your creation with @KalamatasKitchen on Instagram (#KalamatasKitchen).

TOMATES FARCIES **(STUFFED TOMATOES)**

Serves 4

4 medium ripe tomatoes
Fine sea salt and freshly ground white pepper
½ cup fine bread crumbs
1 clove garlic, very finely chopped
1 tablespoon fresh parsley, finely chopped
1 tablespoon fresh basil, finely chopped
½ tablespoon fresh thyme, finely chopped
1 ½ tablespoons grated Parmesan cheese
Extra virgin olive oil
Paring knife
Small spoon
Small mixing bowl
8 x 8″ baking dish

Preheat the oven to 350° F.

Using the paring knife, core the tomatoes. With the small spoon, gently scoop out the center of each tomato and discard. Lightly season the tomatoes with fine sea salt and freshly ground white pepper. In a bowl, mix together the bread crumbs, garlic, parsley, basil, thyme, and Parmesan. Add a splash of olive oil and combine well. Divide the mixture evenly, adding it to the hollow center of the tomatoes, and place them in a baking dish. Place the baking dish in the center of the oven and bake for 30 minutes, or until the mixture is nicely browned and the tomatoes are soft.

Serve immediately. The tomatoes can be stored in the refrigerator for up to 24 hours.

Enjoy!

For more of Chef Eric's delicious recipes perfect for all the Kalamata's Taste Buds go to KalamatasKitchen.com/ripert

LEARN MORE!

PARFAIT

In French, the word *parfait* means "perfect." It's one of Kalamata's favorite words to say when she knows her dish turned out exactly the way she imagined it! In English, *parfait* can also refer to a layered ice-cream dessert served in a fancy tall glass—which is a pretty *parfait* treat, in her opinion!

SOUS CHEF

A sous-chef is one of the most important people in the kitchen. In restaurant kitchens, the sous-chef, or "under-chef," is second in command to the head chef. Every chef appreciates help, and the sous-chef is the chief helper! The next time you're in the kitchen with your own head chef, ask if there is something you can help with. No task is too small for a great sous-chef, and even the smallest task can be the biggest help!

TO CORE

Certain fruits, like apples, pears, and tomatoes have cores that contain the seeds, which you don't usually want to eat. To core a fruit like that is to remove those middle parts. In the case of Chef Eric's *tomates farcies*, it's not that you can't eat the juicy middle parts of the tomatoes—he just cores the tomatoes to make space to add all the other delicious ingredients. Let a grown-up cut the top off a tomato for you, then try to core it with a spoon when you make your own *tomates farcies*!

PISTOU SOUP

Have you ever heard of pistou soup? It's a bright, fresh, traditional soup from Provence, full of veggies and herbs. Head over to our website (KalamatasKitchen.com/ripert) where we have Chef Eric's recipe and more, exclusively for Taste Buds!

ABOUT KALAMATA'S TASTE BUDS

Eric Ripert is the chef and co-owner of the acclaimed New York restaurant Le Bernardin, which holds three Michelin stars and was ranked #1 worldwide by La Liste in 2019. Born in Antibes, France, Ripert moved as a young child to Andorra, where his family instilled in him their own passion for food. At the age of fifteen, he left home to attend culinary school before going on to work in some of the world's most celebrated kitchens. Outside of Le Bernardin, Ripert is the vice chairman of the board of City Harvest, an organization dedicated to rescuing healthy and nutritious food from restaurants and retailers and delivering it to New York's neediest.

Sarah is Kalamata's story-chef, and she also considers herself a professional try-things-twicer. Sarah moved to New York City to join the esteemed Le Bernardin family as a sommelier in 2014. During her time there, she passed the advanced sommelier exam, was featured in the popular *SOMM* film series, and cofounded Kalamata's Kitchen. Her job, no matter the venue, is to create lasting memories by encouraging people to experience the world through food, drink, and community. When she cooks up the adventures of Kalamata and Al Dente, she draws on her own memories in her mother's kitchen.

Jo is the illustrator of Kalamata's adventures and the daughter of an amazing chef. Jo was the kid who would eat anything, and she loves sharing that sense of curiosity and joy for food with her own children, Jude and Oliver. In addition to bringing Kalamata to life, Jo has created the iconic cover art for works such as Glennon Doyle's Love Warrior series, as well as Abby Wambach's *Wolfpack*. You can also find her mural work all over Arlington, Virginia, and Washington, DC, as well as in numerous local restaurants and art studios.

ABOUT KALAMATA'S KITCHEN

Food brings people closer together. And we believe that sharing food adventures does more than encourage your family to try new things—we believe it brings about an appetite for curiosity, courageousness, and compassion in a very simple way: sitting together and connecting over food. Our table is always growing, and we're glad you're a part of what we're cooking up.